Ladybird books are widely available, but in case of
difficulty may be ordered by post or telephone from:

Ladybird Books – Cash Sales Department
Littlegate Road Paignton Devon TQ3 3BE
Telephone 0803 554761

A catalogue record for this book is available
from the British Library

Published by Ladybird Books Ltd Loughborough Leicestershire UK

THE TAILOR OF
GLOUCESTER ™

Based on the original and authorized story
by Beatrix Potter
Ladybird Books in association with Frederick Warne

Ladybird

In the time of swords and periwigs and full-skirted coats with flowered lappets, there lived a tailor in Gloucester. But although he sewed fine silk for his neighbours, he was very, very poor.

One bitter, cold day near Christmas, the tailor began to make a coat – a special coat of cherry-coloured silk. It was going to be the wedding coat for the Mayor of Gloucester who was getting married that very Christmas.

"The finest of wedding coats," said the tailor, "and a cream-coloured satin waistcoat, trimmed with gauze and green chenille."

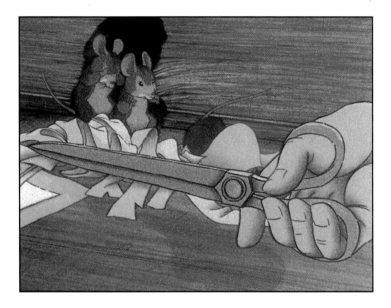

The tailor worked and worked. He
measured the silk and turned it round
and round, trimming it into shape
with his shears. His table and floor
were soon littered with cherry-
coloured snippets, which little brown
mice gathered for their own coats.
"By my whiskers," said one of the
mice, "I cannot remember when we
last had silk of such quality!"

When it grew dark, the tailor left his shop, for he did not sleep there at night. All the silk and satin lay cut out upon the table. There were twelve pieces for the coat and four pieces for the waistcoat. There were pocket flaps and cuffs, and buttons all in order. All was ready to be sewn together in the morning, except the tailor needed one length of cherry-coloured silk thread.

The tailor shuffled slowly home
through the snow leaving the shop
empty except for the little brown mice,
who ran in and out of the shop
without any keys!

Using secret passages and staircases behind the wooden wainscots of all the old houses in Gloucester, they could run from house to house.

Indeed, the little brown mice could run all over the town without ever going into the streets!

The tailor lived alone with his cat, Simpkin, who looked after the house while the tailor was at work. Simpkin was fond of the mice of Gloucester, though he gave them no satin for coats!

"Simpkin old friend," said the tailor, when he arrived home that evening, "we shall make our fortune from this coat, but I am worn to a ravelling.

"Take this, our last fourpence, and a china pipkin," the tailor went on, "and buy a penn'orth of bread, a penn'orth of milk and a penn'orth of sausages. And Simpkin, with the last penny of our fourpence buy me one penn'orth of cherry-coloured silk. But do not lose the last penny, Simpkin, or I am undone, for I have *no more twist*."

"Miaw," said Simpkin, and went out into the dark.

The tailor was very tired and feeling ill. He sat down by the fire and talked to himself about the wonderful coat he was making. He was sure that, at last, he would make his fortune.

"The Mayor has ordered a coat and an embroidered waistcoat – lined with yellow taffeta – and I have just enough material," he said. "There is no more left over in snippets than will serve to make tippets for mice."

On the other side of the kitchen there
was a dresser, and from the dresser
there suddenly came a number of
little noises – *Tip tap, tip tap, tip tap tip!*
"This is very peculiar," said the tailor.
"Whatever can that be?" He crossed
the kitchen and lifted up one of the
teacups that lay upside-down on the
dresser.

Out stepped a little lady mouse, who curtsied to the tailor! Then she hopped down off the dresser, and under the wainscot.

All at once from the dresser there came other little noises – *Tip tap, tip tap, tip tap tip!* "I'll wager this is all Simpkin's doing. The rascal!" said the tailor, and he turned over another teacup.

Out stepped a little gentleman mouse, who bowed to the tailor!

And then from all over the dresser came a chorus of little tappings, and out from under teacups and from under bowls and basins, stepped more little mice who hopped down off the dresser and under the wainscot, too.

The tailor sat down again by the fire, warming his cold hands, and mumbling to himself. "Was I wise to entrust my last fourpence to Simpkin?" he sighed. "One and twenty buttonholes of cherry-coloured silk! To be finished by noon on Saturday, and it is already Tuesday evening! And was it right to let loose those mice, undoubtedly the property of Simpkin?"

The little mice came out from behind
the wainscot and listened to the tailor
as he described the wonderful clothes
he was making for the Mayor.

Suddenly, the mice heard Simpkin
returning with the pipkin of milk, so
they all ran away, squeaking and
calling to one another. Soon, not one
mouse was left in the tailor's kitchen.

"Simpkin," said the tailor, "where is my *twist*?" But Simpkin just looked suspiciously at the dresser. He wanted his supper of little fat mouse! And if he had been able to talk, he would have asked, "Where is my *mouse*?"

Simpkin hid the little parcel of twist in the teapot. He spat and growled at the tailor. "Alack, I am undone!" said the Tailor of Gloucester, and went sadly to bed.

Back in the tailor's shop, the embroidered silk and satin lay cut out upon the table. And who should come to sew them, when the window was barred, and the door was locked?

Why, the little brown mice, who run in and out through all the old houses in Gloucester, without any keys!

The tailor was ill for three days and nights and then it was Christmas Eve, and very late at night.

It is said that all animals can talk in the night between Christmas Eve and Christmas Day – though there are very few folk that can hear them, or know what it is they say!

When the cathedral clock struck twelve, from all the roofs of all the old wooden houses in Gloucester came a thousand merry voices singing old Christmas rhymes.

Simpkin heard the singing and came out of the tailor's home, and wandered about in the snow. He felt hungry, and still wanted his supper of little, fat mice.

Simpkin could see a glow of light from the tailor's shop. He crept up to peep into the window and saw the shop was full of glowing candles. There was a snippeting of scissors, and snappeting of thread, and little mouse voices sang loudly and happily.

"Miaw! Miaw!" cried Simpkin, as he scratched at the shop's door. But the key was under the tailor's pillow, and he could not get in.

The little mice only laughed and sang another tune. Then they sprang to their feet and began to shout all at once in little twittering voices,
"No more twist!
No more twist!"

Simpkin saw what the mice were doing and went home, feeling quite ashamed. He took the little parcel of silk out of the teapot and put it on the tailor's bed.

When the tailor awoke the next morning, the first thing he saw on the patchwork quilt was the parcel of cherry-coloured silk, and beside his bed stood the repentant Simpkin! "Alack, I am worn to a ravelling," said the Tailor of Gloucester, "but I have my twist!"

The tailor got up, dressed and went out into the street with Simpkin running in front of him.

"The Mayor of Gloucester is to be married by noon – and where is his cherry-coloured coat?" muttered the tailor.

He unlocked the shop door and Simpkin ran in. But there was no one there! Not even one little brown mouse!

The tailor gave a shout of joy. "I cannot believe my eyes!" he gasped. "It's a miracle!" There, where he had left the silk, lay the most beautiful coat and embroidered satin waistcoat that ever were worn by a Mayor of Gloucester. There were roses and pansies on the front of the coat, and the waistcoat was covered with embroidered poppies and cornflowers.

Everything was finished, except one single cherry-coloured buttonhole. And pinned to that buttonhole was a scrap of paper with these words in little teeny weeny writing – *NO MORE TWIST!*

From then on the Tailor of Gloucester grew quite stout and quite rich. He made the most wonderful waistcoats for fine gentlemen. Never were seen such ruffles, or such embroidered cuffs and lappets!

But his buttonholes were the greatest triumph of all. The stitches of those buttonholes were *so* small, they looked as if they had been made by little mice!